Puffin Books

GETTING THE STORY

Hurricanes and heroic acts, disasters and discoveries, wars and elections, strange stories, sad ones, happy ones and funny ones – they're all news. And everyone wants to hear news, whether it's good or bad. Each morning, millions of people all over the world switch on the radio or television, and often pick up a newspaper as well. In the last hundred years we have come to expect that whatever happens in the world, we will know about it within a few hours.

But how is it done? How can these stories reach us so quickly? Who are the people who gather the news, and choose which stories are important? What sort of equipment do they need? What are their problems? Could you do a journalist's job, or a news photographer's? *Getting the Story* will tell you this and much more besides.

Libby Purves presents Radio 4's *Midweek*, and writes regularly for *The Times*. She's written and edited several books including *Farming* for Puffin. She lives with her husband, Paul Heiney, and children, Nicholas and Rose, on a working farm in Suffolk.

D0184850

By the same author

FARMING

Libby Purves

Getting the Story

How the news is gathered

Illustrated by
Peter Bull

PUFFIN BOOKS

Thanks to the editors and staff of the *Daily Express*, BBC East and
BBC Radio for their particular help and advice.

PUFFIN BOOKS

Published by the Penguin Group
Penguin Books Ltd, 27 Wrights Lane, London W8 5TZ, England
Penguin Books USA Inc., 375 Hudson Street, New York, New York
  10014, USA
Penguin Books Australia Ltd, Ringwood, Victoria, Australia
Penguin Books Canada Ltd, 10 Alcorn Avenue, Toronto, Ontario,
  Canada M4V 3B2
Penguin Books (NZ) Ltd, 182–190 Wairau Road, Auckland 10,
  New Zealand

Penguin Books Ltd, Registered Offices: Harmondsworth, Middlesex,
  England

Published in Puffin Books 1993
10 9 8 7 6 5 4 3 2 1

Typeset by Datix International Limited, Bungay, Suffolk
Set in 14/15 pt Times
Printed in Great Britain by Clays Ltd, St Ives plc

Contents

1 In the Beginning

Long before radio, television or
newspapers, the only way for news to
travel around was through one person
telling another. If there was a flood,
earthquake or invasion in one part of the
country, the more distant parts did not
know straight away. If a king died or was
overthrown, it often took months for his
subjects in the wilder parts of the nation to
find out they had a new ruler. News was
carried by travellers: wandering friars,
pedlars, pilgrims, or the drovers who walked

great distances with their cattle, sheep, pigs or even geese, taking them to market in the big towns. When a traveller came to a village, everyone would gather round the newcomer and ask: 'What is the news from the North?' or 'What news from London?' They would then pass the news on, and so it spread round the country.

Sometimes musicians, known as minstrels, wrote songs full of news and stories, and these songs travelled far and wide. Of course, the sense of the story often got changed to make a better song, and people would remember bits wrongly so that the news was turned into rumours. Sometimes they wrote out the songs and sold the copies. For many centuries news could only be passed on by word of mouth and handwritten notes.

The first written, public collection of news that we know about was produced in Ancient Rome, in about 50 BC. The senate, who governed the Empire, put together sheets of news called *Acta Diurna* – which means daily business. Scribes wrote out 2,000 copies, which were sent all over the Roman Empire and hung up in market-places and public buildings so that everyone could read them.

Another early way of spreading news was through the town crier. His job was to walk

along the streets, sometimes with a bell,
shouting pieces of news (sometimes he
shouted out the time and the weather as
well. Perhaps you know the Christmas carol
which goes 'Past three o'clock, and a fine
frosty morning': that was a town crier's
call). Of course, the pieces of news had to
be very short.

Find a piece of news in your local paper, or national paper (or just think of some news about your family or your school) and write it out in one or two short sentences. See how it would work if you were a town crier: shout it out!

Now think of the kind of story which someone in a medieval town might like to have known. Perhaps the king's wife has had a son; or there is a shortage of wheat in the next town, so they can't bake bread; or imagine that there has been a disaster, like the Great Fire of London. Try to tell the news as a town crier would. Or write a song about it, and sing the news.

THE EARLY DAYS OF MODERN NEWS

Five hundred years ago, in the fifteenth century, the printing press was invented. The first books were rare and very expensive, but as the presses were developed, people realized they could also publish newspapers and magazines. The first newspapers were published in Germany and Belgium at the beginning of the seventeenth century.

Gradually, the speed of news gathering improved. Faster printing presses were invented, at first powered by steam and later by electricity. The invention of the telegraph and telephone meant that reporters could

send their stories home quickly. Once film
was invented, news could be shown at the
cinema on 'newsreels', and for the first time
ordinary people could see what was
happening in other countries. When radio
broadcasting first began, they were able to
hear the news not long after it had
happened; and with the invention of
television it became possible to watch scenes
from around the world right in your own
home.

Nowadays we take it for granted that we
can turn on the world's news like a tap, at

any time of the day or night. Some people thought that the coming of radio and television would mean the end of newspapers, but it hasn't: newspapers have become faster and cleverer at getting stories and photographs, and taken advantage of the fact that they can give a lot more detail than broadcast news has time for. Today newspapers, radio and television are all popular. They are great rivals, each newspaper, TV or radio station competing to see who can get a story first, and tell it in the best way. Journalism is a very exciting profession.